THIS K-9 OF MINE

*Poetic short stories from a dog's point of view,
plus a few from the owner's vantage point too.*

By
Jerry Wayne Baldwin

I simply like to give dogs a voice in this world and try
to think what they would say. Thank you for being dog
crazy with me!

-Jerry Wayne Baldwin

WHAT PEOPLE ARE SAYING ABOUT JERRY'S POEMS:

If you have a dog, this is a book for you. The poems can simultaneously bring a smile and a tear along with them. If you've ever stopped and looked at your best friend lying next to you and were overwhelmed with how much you love them, you'll love this book.

-Amazon Customer

I laughed, I cried and smiled all the way through this book! Short read. So worth the money. Want to share with so many people. Buy this book!! It's one of the cutest books written. I promise!

-Mart

Such a fine collection of poetry, told with true passion from the heart of the author.

-Sooz

3

Cover designed by Cover Designer

This book is a work of fiction. Names, characters, places, and incidents either are products of the author's imagination or are used fictitiously. Any resemblance to actual persons, living or dead, events, or locales is entirely coincidental.

Jerry Wayne Baldwin
Visit my website at https://amazon.com/author/jerrywaynebaldwin

Printed in the United States of America

First Printing: Nov 2018
ISBN - 13:978-1-5219-7258-8

CONTENTS

BORDER COLLIE BLUES

I THINK I'M GOING CRAZY. I've never felt this way.
It all started when I got a new dog and brought him home that day.
The breeder warned me about him. Said they're kind of hard to raise.
They take a lot of your time and quite a mess they make.

I just smiled and shook his hand and tucked him under my arm.
I thought, "how could this little black and white pup be of any harm?"
I put him in the back seat as I rolled back into town.
I kept hearing a chewing noise, so I stopped and looked around.

This pup had chewed my seatbelt totally in two,
and had started on the floormats and one of my kids' old shoes.
I got out and picked him up and brought him up with me.
As I started to drive off, he crawled under my seat.

I heard that sound of chewing again, but this time it was underneath.
I stopped again and found him with a bottle cap between his teeth!
I was totally baffled; I didn't know what to do.
Anywhere I put him all he did was chew.

Luckily there was a store nearby, I ran in and got a bone,
hoping it would last until I finally got him home.
He destroyed the bone before I got home, I knew it wouldn't last.
I finally got home and let him run and man that dog is fast!

He ran for what seemed like hours. He just wouldn't quit,
And this dog is very smart; he already learned to sit.
Finally, 4 hours later I took the pup inside.
He explored the whole house and found everywhere to hide.

He took a little power nap for 20 minutes or so,
then he was scratching at the door, telling me he needed to go.
I grabbed up fourteen tennis balls, 6 Frisbees, and a rope.
Maybe all of this will wear him out; it was my only hope.

I started slinging Frisbees; he really had a knack.
He loved taking them away, but never gave them back!
Then I slung the tennis balls; he's the best catcher there ever was.
Once he got a hold of them, he chewed off all the fuzz.

Finally, he was tired, and I laid him in his bed,
in case he got lonely, I laid stuffed animals at his head.
I sat there and watched him as he drifted off to sleep.
I was thinking to myself "Have I gotten in too deep?"

I went into my bedroom and fell asleep right away
and woke up 6 hours later much to my dismay.
I walked into my new friend's room but didn't see my pup.
All I saw was everything the varmint had torn up.

He tore up the stuffed animals and pulled the stuffing out,
and shredded all my pillows and threw them all about.
He chewed up every electric cord to everything I owned.
No lamp, no TV, no stereo; he even chewed my phone!

I went into the kitchen and there the culprit was.
I was going to take him back, this destructive ball of fuzz.
I picked him up and immediately headed for the car.
Put him beside me, started it up, but I didn't get very far.

That's where I made my mistake that day and it was of the biggest size.
I allowed myself to stop right there and look into those eyes.
Those eyes that have the look of love like no other breed.
Those looks of love only Border Collies give is what we really need!

He can't help that he was bred this way, he has a job to do.
And everyone has habits that make them hard to live with too.
Maybe this little runner is a blessing in disguise.
He can help me be more active and maybe lose a couple of pants size!

As for the chewing and destruction, maybe it won't last long.
I can head to the pet store right now and purchase 15 Kongs!
After all, this little guy needs me; I can be his very best friend,
And be with him for his entire life, right 'til the very end!

THE BATH

I HEAR A SOUND THAT'S FAMILIAR. No, I don't like it at all.
Droplets of water splashing like a deep woods waterfall.
It's coming from that room down the hallway. The one dad calls his retreat.
Where that fun roll of paper hangs on the wall and there is a handle on the back of the seat.

Here comes mom with that look in her eyes. This is not going to be fun.
I have only one option left. Excuse me while I take off and ruuuuuunnn!!
The kids are trying to catch me. Mom has her track shoes on too.
This event happens every time I roll around in deer poo!

Oh no they have me cornered. I'm just not gonna budge.
Now they are dragging me like a prisoner going before the judge.
They strip me of my collar and grab me and toss me in!
And use about 13 different concoctions, one, which is tingling my skin.

Mom looks me straight in the eye and says, "Boy I don't understand.
When the kids are in their wading pool you jump in anytime you can."
She just doesn't understand. It's because I am not being forced,
And that's my chance to get even for this, as I shake and make mom wet of course!

She is really digging hard; that deer poo has really set up.
I must admit one thing; I was really one smelly pup.
Oh, I'm not quite done fighting. Just timing my move just right.
Now that I am all lathered up, it's time to make my flight.

She reaches for the sprayer. Mom you just messed up.
Out of the tub I take off running. No one can hold this slippery pup!

Now dad just got involved, running from him is always hard.
My fight is over; I surrender. Dad is covered in soap too.
I guess he will already smell good if he wants to roll in some poo!!!

Dad carries me over to the wading pool. Drops me in and holds me down.

There will probably be pictures of this circus circulating around the town.

Mom has 27 towels out and probably needs a few more.

I'm not quite sure which is wetter, my dad or the kitchen floor!

I am glad this fiasco is over. I hope it doesn't happen again soon.

I think I have learned my lesson this time as I eyeball another pile of poo!!

OLE ROY

WE ALL HAVE THAT "LOOK". Sort of a bond you see.
The same look I see in you, you also see in me!
The look of a dog owner is exactly what I mean,
from the mud on our shoes to the holes in our jeans!

Bloodshot eyes, uncombed hair, rain poncho by the door for us to wear!
Lint rollers laying around for everyone to use, if a sweater with no fur is for that day what we choose.

I guess that works both ways, a hassle for the dog too.
If one of his buds at the dog park says, hey man you have human hair on you!
Getting clothes out of the dryer is always a treat, when that dog snack you left in your pocket now looks like minced meat.

It's really worse than when I was married, the little things I have to do.
Instead of leaving the seat down, now it's the seat and the potty lid too!
The one time I forget to do it this part really is the worst.
I hear the sound of glug, glug, glug, as Ole Roy is quenching his thirst!

I run in to catch him in the act, as I scream, " Come on man!"
While I wipe up the excess dribble, he's in the kitchen going through the trash can!
As I pry the can of ravioli from his mouth, he wants to play tug of war.
As the last piece of Chef Boy Ardee ends up on my just mopped floor!

That's it I am going to take a nap. Some alone time is what I need.

As he rams his head into the door, this dog must always be near me!

I open the door just a little; he gives me that look we all know.

That look that pierces every dog lover's heart and deep into your spirit it goes.

It's as if he is saying I'm sorry, I never mean any harm.

Can I jump up in your bed and snuggle in your arms?

We fall asleep together; a dog lover's heart is true.

As I try to get rejuvenated and prepare for round number two!

THE BEST THINGS IN LIFE

IT'S A DIFFERENT KIND OF MORNING HERE, something must be up.
Everyone is acting very strange, can't get one over on this pup!
Dad just came up from the basement with these plastic long-handled tools,
And the kids are happy and excited, when they should be getting ready for school!

No, this is not a normal day. The TV keeps playing the same old thing,
Talking about a frontal system and the weather it will bring.
Whatever it is, they can have it. I don't care what the weatherman said.
Can someone take me potty, so I can get back in my bed?

They're all busy watching TV. I'll try scratching at the door.
Somebody better come open this or I'm going to go here on the floor!
Finally, Mom to the rescue; she opens the door and lets me fly.
Brrrr, it's awful cold today and somewhat cloudy outside.

There's something tickling my nose today, while I squat to do my biz.
It feels like frozen cotton balls. I wonder what it is.
Now there's stuff falling from the sky. Mom, what could this be?
It's starting to turn the grass all white and sticking to the trees.

There's something magical about this stuff. It makes me want to run!
Run real fast and slam on the brakes, this slippery stuff is fun!
This magical stuff is awesome and makes everybody smile.
Everyone but Dad; he must drive in it for miles.

Even he came out to watch me, "Hey Dad, watch this trick",
I can slide forever in this white stuff that is slick.
I wonder what might happen, if I took a little taste?
Brrr, that stuff just froze my tongue, time for another race!

This time I'll run in circles. It's starting to get deep.
Look at those funny shoes my mom has on her feet!
Now it's coming down harder, getting rather deep.
Kids are lying on flat things on their belly, going down our driveway that is steep!

Dad just picked some of it up and molded it in his hand.
He just threw a snowball at mom!!! Run as fast as you can!
Mom got that determined look and made a big snowball too,
I know how far she can throw tennis balls and that's not good for you!

Now the kids are rolling it up into a giant ball.
They said they're going to build a snowman, at least six feet tall!
Mom just yelled, "come inside" let's take some time to thaw.
As we were heading in, dad threw one last snowball!

As I got warm I was thinking, of how we all had such a fun time.
And the best part about it -- it didn't cost a dime.
The best things in life you can't pay for, like family, friendship, and love.
And fun times on snowy days and blessings from God above!

So, during this season of spending, remember the best gifts are free.
And try to do more of your spending, with loved ones and family!

WINDOWS IN HEAVEN

IT'S MY FIRST DAY IN HEAVEN and what a beautiful place.
You'll be glad to know there's a smile upon my face.
The moment I left you, two angels in white
carried me up here to Heaven that night.

All those stories you hear about Rainbow Bridge are true,
but you don't walk over it, the angels carried me through.
There's a gate at the end made of real pearl.
It must be the biggest gate in the world!

Once I got in and started looking around,
you just won't believe all the things that I found!
The first place they took me had to be the most fun,
a humongous field with miles and miles to run!

Once I was tired, the angels said, "we'll take you to your home,
but first, we need to stop by this place, full of tasty bones."
They told me to take some with me, but one is all I need.
Because every good thing lasts forever, up in heaven, you see.

They took me to my new house. It took my breath away.
The most beautiful place I've ever seen with a huge yard in which to play.
They said, "Come on, let's go inside and have a look around".
They took me to the bottom floor. You won't believe what I found!

The bottom of my house is a window and you won't believe the view.
You see my house sits right over yours, so I can still keep an eye on you!

I was so worried about you when I went away,
now I can watch you every second and know that you are okay!
I can't wait for that moment when we can walk around this place,
and I can cover you with puppy kisses, on every inch of your face!

ALWAYS IN MY WAY

THIS GERMAN SHEPHERD IS driving me nuts.
Always in the way, and up my butt!
Even when I only move two feet away,
he has to be beside me, he just won't stay!

Then he stands sideways in the hallway, I can't get by!
Probably easier to go under, his back is so high.
Then the funniest thing I've ever seen him do,
happens when he's nodding off, trying to take a snooze.

His feet start twitching when he is asleep.
Everybody watch him, don't make a peep.
Then his foot bumps into the hallway door,
makes him jump, straight up in the floor!

Who goes there? Watchdog on call!!
The only intruder is HIM! Bumping the doorway in the hall!
He barks for an hour, he's doing his job.
No bad guys are coming into this place to rob!

He doesn't realize that HE made the noise.
He just wants to find those imaginary burglar boys.
Then I thought about it and the way he is.
What if someone really did sneak in?

That bark would alert me, bless their poor soul.

I feel sorry for them if they get near his food bowl!

So, the next time I complain of him being in the way.

I'll try to remember he might save my life one day!

Thank you, Mr. Shepherd, for being in my way ALL the time!

THE GIFT

'TWAS THE NIGHT BEFORE CHRISTMAS at the SPCA.
No one was stirring or wanting to play.
We were all just sitting there biding our time;
the Bassett Hound beside me was just about blind.

I tried to help the old guy as much as I could,
hoping that Santa knew that I had been good.
The only thing I wanted for Christmas this year
was a nice, warm home with plenty of cheer.

See the owner I had somehow lost his job,
and our new landlord was kind of a snob.
He told my owner, I don't allow pets,
so, I ended up here, where it's cold, dark and wet.

My first night in here was the worst you see,
all the other dogs were snarling at me.
Then they put me in here with Jake; he's my friend.
He is very old, he said he was ten!

He told me all about the man that wears black.
He takes pets outside, but they never come back.
It scares me so much when I see him walk by.
We all go to the back of our cages and hide.

I think about my owner a lot. I miss him so much.
The sound of his voice, his most gentle touch.
A home for Christmas would be a dream come true.
And since I'm wishing big, how about a home for Jake too!

I heard people talking about a tree down at the mall,
that had pictures of us on it, and a number they could call.
I hope somebody wants me. I would be such a good pet.
And I got all my shots last month down at the vet.

It's starting to get dark outside, it's just about that time,
when they fill up all our water bowls and hang up the CLOSED sign.
I guess my wish isn't happening. It was too good to be true.
Wait, what's that sound I hear? Jake said he hears it too!

I hear people talking. Could they be coming after me?
After all I looked really handsome, in that picture on the adoption
tree!
Look Jake, the door is opening, many people are here.
Hopefully to take us to a new home, with lots of Christmas cheer.

It's true, we are all getting new homes, the greatest gift of all.
I hope they have some Frisbees and lots of tennis balls.
Everyone had their minds made up, on which dog they would take.
We all got picked and taken outside. Everyone but Jake.

This just can't be happening. I can't leave him all alone.
He always took good care of me, even shared his Milk bones.
Then a Christmas miracle happened, right before my eyes.

Jake's Christmas wish was granted, under the starry sky.

Santa Claus showed up that night, but he wasn't in a sleigh.
He came to adopt my friend that night, in a beat-up Chevrolet!
Jake didn't care what he was driving. He was happy as could be,
to think that someone would still want him, even though he couldn't see!

That's how the story ended. See wishes do come true.
So, make sure you're being nice this year, 'cause Santa Claus is watching you!

50 QUESTIONS

MR. GERMAN SHEPHERD THERE ARE SOME THINGS I NEED TO KNOW and only you can tell me. Here's question #1. Let's go.

Why do you insist on being in my way? No matter what I do.
You lay there in the doorway, never letting me through.
Then right when I step over you, you start to stand up, of course.
Then I'm straddling you between my legs, like a jockey on a horse.

As I dismount and head to the kitchen, you must be in the lead.
You must be a NASCAR fan or have watched 'Need for Speed'.
I finally make it to the kitchen; it must be time to eat.
Why do you never get filled up with all that food and those treats?

Then it's time for water. This is the part you like best.
I've never seen any other breed make as much of a mess!
It's like you just hold it in your mouth and swish it all around.
Then you start to walk away and spit it on the ground.

Then when it's almost empty, you do this trick that's neat.
You step into your water bowl splashing with all four feet.
Another thing I must ask, I need to know this and more.
Why won't you ever move when I try to open the door?

You lay there and look up at me like you just don't have a care.

I know there are other doors in this house. I will use the one over there!

Then there is this weird thing you twist and turn your head.

And give this really puzzled look, like you can't figure out what I said!

Then it's time to potty, my favorite time of day.

Walking around with plastic bags on my hands, listening to what my neighbors say!

This is nothing personal. Please don't take this wrong,

But you bark at things that aren't there or at least when I look they are gone!

Mr. Shepherd, I love you. You're well worth everything I give.

If I could I would change but one thing about you, that's the number of years you live!

MR. SHEPHERD REPLIES, a lot of questions you have asked. All of them I have answers for today.

The first thing that you wanted to know, is why I lay in your way?
My main job in life is to protect you, that's what I do best, you see.
If anyone wants to get to you, they must go through me!

Then you asked why I like to be first, everywhere we go.
Well, I am so handsome. I make a great first impression;
I can't help it you're so slow.

Then you asked why I eat so much and when I eat why I take so long.

Look if I am to be your protector, I need all the food I can get to help make me strong.

Then you asked about this problem I have with spitting water all over the floor.

Well if I drank it all, as much as I pee, I'd have to live outdoors!

Then you wondered why it is; I splash water like I just don't care.

I'm just showing you where you need to mop. See you missed a spot right there.

Then you asked why I won't move when you try to open the door.

Hey, it took me 2 hours to get comfortable; you try lying on this hard floor.

Then you brought up the subject of why I tilt my head.

Well, I love you so much; I just want to understand everything you said.

Then you had to mention potty time and why it smells so bad.

It has to do with that Blue Buffalo and all those bully sticks I had.

You're the one following me around, picking it up with those gloves that are blue.

Maybe you should get another hobby. I seriously worry about you!

Then you inquired about my barking. Well, I hear things you can't see.

I won't let anyone near our house and I am cheaper than ADT!

Well I answered all your questions about the strange things I do.

Please remember the most important thing, I will always love you!

LETTING GO

(Dedicated to everyone facing the challenge of "letting go".)

THANK YOU FOR SPENDING your life with me.
The great times will not be forgotten.
I hope you will always think of me as the one who spoiled you rotten.

You were always by my side. With you, I was never alone.
Now it's my turn to be by your side,
as you take your final journey home.

See, God only keeps you here a little while
and I'm glad you spent it with me.
But your past year has been a bit rough, as everyone could see.

But you were strong and courageous, and never left my side.
I saw everything you were going through,
that pain you could never hide.

You've been the best friend I could ask for, you never asked for much.
When I was down or even sick, you provided the gentlest touch.

Your journey isn't over yet. You're going where there is no pain.
I know this humongous loss for me, will be all of Heaven's gain.

I will be right here as you cross over, and be praying to God above,
To hold you in his arms tonight and give you lots of love.

I will even remind him of all your favorite things.
So, you will have plenty to keep you busy, as you listen to the Angels sing.

Well, it's time now and it's killing me, this pain, it cuts so deep.
I must remember you're not gone forever, you're just going to sleep.

Do me one favor if you don't mind and save a place for me!
But the thing I want for you the most is to run free precious one, run free!

TWO HEROES

I WAS LOOKING TO GET A NEW PUP.
So, I asked my very best friend. He said get a German Shepherd;
they are loyal til the end.

He sent me to this breeder he knew. I went over to his home.
He had a litter of brown and black pups in a large pen is where they
roamed.

I didn't know a lot about the breed, but I did see one in the park.
He always guarded the water bowl and had a real loud bark!

I asked him lots of questions, this breeder knew his stuff.
He picked up one in particular and said this guy is really tough.

He rambled on about West Germans and working stock and coats.
I just wanted a new best friend; I could take with me on my boat.

The breeder warned me about them, said they are kind of hard to
raise.
He said they shed like crazy and quite a mess they make.

And don't be mad if he wakes you up when he hears funny sounds.
He just wants to protect you from strangers that might be around.

I made up my mind to do it. I want this little pup.
But I didn't know how much money, I was going to have to give up!

I gave the man his money, but didn't get very far.
Before thought came to me, this dog cost more than my first car!

I put him in the back seat. I didn't bring a crate.
He slept most of the way home; raising him is a piece of cake.

Then I heard a whimper, which turned into a whine.
Then I witnessed the worst smell ever, since the very beginning of time.

I don't know how to describe it. Smelled something like the zoo,
mixed with a porta potty, and my ex-wife's homemade stew.

This little guy had pottied all over my seat.
Then he peed on my floorboard as an extra little treat.

Luckily, I was almost home. I had all the windows down.
My car smelled like the trash truck, that makes its way through town.

I got home and grabbed the dog and put him in the pen.
Then I noticed him standing real funny, oh no, he is pooping again!

I didn't have time to get it up. I had a mess to clean.
This boy could make more mess than any dog I had ever seen.

An hour later I was finished, I went back to the pen.
The smell I had just gotten rid of, there it was again!

I didn't have time to clean it; my new friend wanted to play.

This guy was truly smart; he already learned to stay.

He liked this big rope I had and loved to play tug of war.
Then I got out the tennis ball, which he loved even more.

I slung the ball as far as I could. The best fetcher there ever was.
The part he liked about it the most was chewing off the fuzz.

Then we stopped for water; I filled the bowl to the top.
Sloppiest drinker I had ever seen. Looked like a pig eating slop.

Most of the water just stayed in his mouth and trickled down his chin.
Then he dove in for more, and did it, again and again!

The bowl was almost empty. Most of it was on the ground.
Then he jumped in with all four paws and splashed it all around.

I said, "that's it, let's go inside. I'll show you where to sleep.
But before you crash I guess I better, get you something to eat."

I filled his bowl up to the top. He attacked it like a wolf on its prey.
Then he growled and snarled when I tried to take it away.

After that I put him to bed and we both laid down to sleep.
I lay there, eyes open, thinking I have gotten in too deep!

Maybe I should have thought this through and purchased a different breed.
He eats so much and poops a ton; this isn't what I really need.

Finally, I had just dozed off, was sleeping quite well.
Then I heard my new pup barking, at the front door, I could tell.

He was barking loudly and scratching at the door.
I told him to just calm down. He began barking even more.

He was trying to tell me something, in the middle of that night.
Something only he could hear, that wasn't in my sight.

Finally, he convinced me. So, I looked outside.
Looking out the window, I saw a man trying to hide.

I grabbed my phone and called police, they showed up right away.
They said a guy had broken out of jail, earlier that day.

There must have been 14 police cars and one of them said K9.
Out jumped a 100-pound dog, a bigger version of mine!

They caught the guy and took him in and locked him up real tight.
Then the thought crossed my mind; there were two Shepherd heroes that night!

HOW THE BC SAVED CHRISTMAS

'TWAS THE NIGHT BEFORE CHRISTMAS in a Border Collie's house.

Not a creature was stirring, not even a mouse.

The puppy was excited about what lay in store.

When he jumped up in the window, the tree hit the floor.

His owners ran down to see what was the matter,

when they entered the room, they stepped on balls that were shattered!

For the third time that day they cleaned up this mess,

that was caused by the little black and white pest.

After they cleaned up, they all went to bed,

as visions of pig ears danced in the pup's head.

When out on the lawn, there arose a loud clatter,

the collie jumped up in the window to see what was the matter.

What he saw when he looked really blew him away,

eight tiny reindeer had come over to play.

He ran through the kitchen and out the dog door,

and past a chubby little man, a red suit he wore.

He barked at the deer and they started to run.

Then he herded them back, now this was real fun!

The chubby little man had entered their home,
while the border and reindeer continued to roam.
When the pup realized the guy in red was nowhere to be found;
he sniffed him out like the best bloodhound.
He looked inside and sure enough he was there,
filling up everyone's stockings with care.

He was dressed all in red with a little white trim,
and had ashes and soot all over him!
He had red cheeks and a little round belly,
  that shook when he laughed like a bowl full of jelly.
He patted the pup on top of his head,
and told him he needed to get back in his bed.

The pup listened well like most Border Collies do,
and ran up the steps until Santa was through.
The pup tried to sleep but kept hearing a noise.
It seemed Santa was having a hard time with those reindeer boys.
Santa saw the pup in the window with a frown;
so, he motioned with his hand for him to come down.

He told the pup his reindeer were rowdy this year,
and not being able to finish was his biggest fear.
They seemed to act well for this Border Collie pup,
so, he asked him to ride along as they went up.
The deer straightened up when they heard that thought.
They can't run away now, they will surely be caught!

Then Santa tossed the boy an all-natural treat,
and with one swift jump he was up in the seat.
He put the reigns into the yappy pup's mouth,
and said, "you guide the sled, we are heading down south".
Then Santa yelled up, up, and away,
and that's how the Border Collie saved Christmas day!

When the presents were all delivered,
and Santa's work was through,
he laid the tired pup in his bed at home,
while his mommy and daddy snoozed!

DOG'S BEST FRIEND

SO SORRY I NEED TO GO OUTSIDE SO MUCH.
The years seem to have caught up with me.
You are the most understanding owner,
taking me out at 3:00 a.m. to pee.

My best years are now behind me. I don't get around well these days.
I used to always want to stay outside, but lately inside is where I stay.

Sorry for the extra vet visits. My body is wearing out fast.
Thank you for staying by my side. How did ten years just pass?

Remember the day you brought me home? I was the apple of your eye!
You gave me the best life I could imagine. Life really does seem to fly by!

My mind is full of many great memories,
like those weekends down at the lake.
I hate the thought of moving on without you,
not sure how much more my body can take.

If there is one thing I want you to know, as my earthly life comes to an end.
I love you more than words can say.
You're not just my owner; you're my lifelong best friend!

MY PROM DATE

HOURS AND HOURS OF TRAINING I'VE HAD to do a special job.
I am what they call a service dog, excuse me while I pull this knob.
Maggie is my special friend; she is in a metal chair.
Excuse me I will be right back, she needs a brush for her hair.

See Maggie's legs don't work real well. She had an accident when she was nine.
Was hurt really bad in a swimming pool, they said she broke her spine.
That's when I came to live here, so glad they needed me.
Sounds like she's having a problem, hang on, let me go see.

It was really nothing; just her spoon hit the floor.
Then she wanted to go outside, so I opened up her door.
I came here to live eight years ago, everyone was so upset.
Once everything settled down, they were the nicest people I ever met.

Maggie's getting her hair done today. I've been there before.
That's the place where people get their toes scrubbed, and there's hair all over the floor.
Her mom is taking us down there; there's some kind of event tonight.
I will just tag along behind and try to stay out of sight.

Lots of people at the hair place today. Something must be up.
The sign on my back says dog at work, don't try to pet this pup!
Finally, we are out of there, one more place to go.
She's picking up a really pretty dress and a tie shaped like a bow.

I am glad Maggie's smiling today. She had been a bit down.
Amazing how a mani/pedi can wipe away a frown!!!
Finally back home, I'll get that door. Can I help with anything else?
Yes, I remember where your phone is. I will get it off that shelf.

I heard her talking to her friends about where they would meet.
I think she has a date tonight, she didn't ok that with me!
I'll admit it I am jealous. I worry about my girl.
I've always taken care of her. She really is my world.

Everyone is meeting here tonight. I can't wait to meet this guy.
He'd better be really nice to her or I'll give him a black eye!
All her friends are here now. They're all with their dates.
Maggie's guy is nowhere to be found. I figured he would be late.

Then they started taking pictures in front of the old willow tree.
She pulled out that tie shaped like a bow, then she put it on ME!!
That made me so happy. Look how handsome I am mom.
Me and my precious Maggie are going to the prom!

I danced every dance that night with Maggie she's my girl.
She may never walk again, but she's the best dancer in the world!

WITHOUT YOU

IT'S MY FIRST CHRISTMAS WITHOUT YOU; there's a void in my heart.
I was always the apple of your eye, and I was right from the start.
From the very first time I brought you home, til I laid you down to rest,
You were always by my side, simply put, you were the best.

I miss that look that you would give, when you knew I had a treat.
And the way I always felt secure, with your head on top of my feet.
Christmas time was always special, our favorite time of year.
Full of treats and toys and gifts, and hearts full of cheer.

But this year is very different, unlike any Christmas I've ever had.
Instead of having a blast with you, I'm lonely and I'm sad.
I even hung your stocking up, the same place it was before.
And put your picture in a wreath and hung it on the door.

Christmas time in heaven as you decorate God's throne.
Hope he gives you all your heart's desires, and lots of marrow bones.
Yes, it's my saddest Christmas ever; really wishing you were here.
Wagging your tail, giving me hugs, and licking away my tears!

'TIL WE MEET AGAIN

PLEASE DON'T CRY BECAUSE I LEFT YOU. I simply had a job to do.
I had to cross over to heaven, to get things ready for you.
If anyone in the world knows you, it would certainly be me.
Look at all those hours I spent laying at your feet.

God only puts us together for a little while and, of me, you were always so proud.
Down there is where I stole your heart away. Up here we will dance on the clouds.
I am already staying at your mansion; there are other animals here too.
All of us have one thing in common; we had the best owner ever....YOU!

I am not sure when we will meet again; each day down there is a gift.
I am waiting with anticipation, to give you your first heavenly puppy kiss!
There is one sure way to mend your heartache and to keep you from being so sad,
go find another pup eventually, give them the same special life I had!

Thank you for making my life with you special every single day.
Like always, I will meet you at the front door when God brings you up this way!!!

THE V E T!!!

SOMETHING MUST BE UP TODAY. Everyone is acting strange.

Mom is talking to everyone in codes. Spelling out three letter names.

Does she really not know I can spell? Maybe I should remind her again.

Every dog in the world knows V-E-T, means place that sticks you with pins!

I gotta find some place to hide. Mom's going crazy, she's got it bad.

Following me all around the backyard, putting my poop in a clear bag!!!!

She has a folder full of papers; on it is my name.

She has the leash hooked tightly, I guess I'll go along with her game.

She puts me in the back of her SUV. She floors it, man she can fly.

As I look back in the picture window, Mr. Kitty cat is waving bye bye!

We get to this weird looking building; I have been through this drill before.

Where all the animals growl at each other, and someone usually pees on the floor.

The vet is kinda busy today. That looks strange, what the heck?

How in the world did that happen, that Beagle has a funnel around his neck?

I asked him, how did he get this way? I couldn't believe what he said.

He said they chopped off these things that were making him mean and threw them away instead!

That's it. I gotta make a break. Oh no, they just called my name.

What if they chop something off me? I will never be the same!

They dragged me to the back of this place, onto something called a scale.

Mom tells them all about me. I'm a two year old, unaltered male!

Now they want to take my temperature. You want to put that thing where?

I don't see that happening bud, as my mom just sits in that chair.

A lot of help she is holding that baggie full of my poo!

If I ever go with you to your vet, see if I try to help you!!

Now they are talking in codes together, something about D H L P.

I think all that translates into a needle is going in me!!

A lady walks into the room with a smile on her face.

She says baby this won't hurt a bit! They sure lie a lot in this place!

She grabs the fur behind my neck. I have been through this before.

I will get even with you smiley lady, I'm going to pee right on your floor!

Mom screams oh gosh, I am sorry! I am peeing and I just can't stop.

Maybe miss smiley lady should trade that needle for a mop.

Mom drags me out to the checkout desk. They said my sample was fine.

She makes an appointment and pays the fee, says I will see you all next time!

I bet they remember me for a long time. I left that exam room a wreck.

I am glad I got out with nothing being chopped and no funnel around my neck!!

———————————●———————————

THE TREE

MY DAD SHOULD BE HOME FROM WORK HERE SOON. I always meet him at the door.
He likes it when I give him high fives, puppy kisses, and more!

I just heard a car door slam. I think it could be him!
I hope he brought me a pig ear, or a pack of puppy Slim Jims.

The door is opening slowly, he yells, "Everybody outside!"
What? No pig ear or puppy treats? But a much bigger surprise.

There's a tree tied on the roof of my daddy's SUV.
That thing is huge, I hope it doesn't come tumbling down on me!

This is the day we decorate the tree. I remember from last year.
We played music, mom cooked a roast, and there was lots of Christmas cheer.

Dad and my brothers had a time getting it in the door.
By the time they stood it up, it was almost six feet four!

My sister was bringing up boxes from the basement down below,
With lots of sparkling tinsel and candles we can show.

Then dad took his finger and pointed straight at me.
He said your job from this moment on is keeping the cat out of this tree!

I took that job serious, but he was sneaky as can be.
One night he was drinking my water and eating my jerky treats!

I hear Mom in there cooking, gosh, it smells so good.
The house is very warm with the fireplace full of wood!

Everyone is decorating. It's over halfway through.
Mr. Fluffkins stay out of that tree, I have a job to do!

We have awesome decorations for everyone to see.
Balls and bells and ribbons and one with a picture of me!

Dad said "now for the best part…" it's in the trunk of Moms car.
He ran outside and came back in with a beautiful shining star!

Then dad said, "Who should put it on top?" I was hoping they would say me.
Then everyone said, "let's let mom put it on top of the tree!"

She stood on a chair and did it. Finally, it was done.
That six foot four Fraser fir was the center of our fun.

Magnificent in all its glory, that tree was really the best.
Something to show off to family, friends, and guests.

Then a thought came to my mind, I thought about last year.
About when Christmas was over, beginning a new year.

Last year's tree was beautiful, but when it stopped being fun,
After everyone received their gifts and all the unwrapping was done.

We stripped off all the pretty things, that tree of over 6 feet.
Roughly drug it down the driveway and tossed it beside the street.

Then I thought of people treated the same way.
Once their glitter and worth were gone, they just get thrown away.

Think of someone in your life you've not heard from in a while.
Send a card, make a call. Go that extra mile.

Inside, that person is still as beautiful as when they were in their prime.
Go tell them that you love them, while you still have time!

Merry Christmas!

MISSING YOU

WHAT AM I SUPPOSED TO DO about the empty space here on my bed?

And what about this special pillow where you used to lay your head?

What about all these squeak toys that got on my nerves all the time?

I wish you were still here to chew them that would be soothing to these ears of mine.

And what about this food bowl? For years it's been here on the floor.

I can't bring myself to put it away; my heart is just way too torn!

I messed up today as I went outside. It really was a shame.

I am so used to you going out with me; I actually called out your name.

Even the mailman is missing you. He stopped by on his route today.

Said he noticed the window was empty in that favorite spot where you laid.

Even he got teary eyed. Sometimes your name he would call.

I guess that's proof right there that you really were loved by all!

Lost is the way I feel right now. I never knew I could feel this bad.

It was the hardest thing I've ever done, letting go of the best friend I had.

The memories we had are so special and the pictures are way too few.

If I could have but ONE prayer answered, it would be ONE MORE DAY WITH YOU!

CHANGES

This is for everyone that is missing summer already!

SOMEONE IS PLAYING A TRICK ON ME like nothing I have ever seen.
Seems like yesterday the trees were full and our backyard was green.
The sun stayed out forever. I was splashing in a kiddie pool.
Yes, someone is playing a trick on me. I am nobody's fool!

The weekends are really different now. Dad has put away his grill.
He used to slip me pieces of smoked chicken that was my summer thrill.
The sun used to stay out forever, now some days it won't even show.
Yes, someone is playing a trick on me. I miss those days watching dad mow.

What happened to all the birds that were here? Now there are only a few.
And those green bugs that made a buzzing noise, that mainly showed up in June!
And those puffy flowers kids would blow on making helicopters fly;
Same flowers dad would mow, over three times, as he yelled and screamed! Oh my!

Yes, someone is playing a trick on me. The kids used to be here all day.
Now they climb in a yellow tank in the mornings, that takes them all away.
I'd watch in the window, missing them bad. Hoping they'll be home soon.
They're always in a bad mood in the mornings, but laughing in the afternoon!

Yes, I do miss summer. I wish it were here all year.
Especially here in the winter, when snow and sleet are near.
Then I heard my mom explain it. It was no trick at all.
Just life and the change of seasons, winter, spring, summer and fall.

Our lives are always changing, just like the seasons do.
Enjoy each season for what it is, life is precious, it ends too soon.
If it were summer every day, then it too would get old.
I do appreciate summer more, now that it's bitter and cold.

There's beauty in every season in life, even when things seem bad.
When things get tough, keep in mind, all the good seasons you've had.
Whatever trial you are facing today, don't let it under your skin.
This day only lasts 24 hours, and then you will NEVER see it again!

Dedicated to everyone struggling with the seasons of life!

THE RIDE

I HEARD FIVE OF MY FAVORITE WORDS TODAY, my emotions I cannot hide.

I always get really excited, when mom says, "Let's go for a ride!"
She opens the door, puts on my leash, and yells c'mon boy jump up.
Got the whole backseat to myself. I love this life of a spoiled pup!

Mom gets in and cranks up her van. It's time for me to explore.
Jackpot! Only one minute in and I find beef jerky on the floor!!
Mom turns around and says, "What's in your mouth?" You give that to me!
There's no way I am giving this up. It's delicious as can be!

I swallow just as fast as I can, as we are heading down the road.
I gotta get over to the window and go into search mode!
I like to look for other dogs that are riding with their owners too.
I think I just saw a Bassett Hound in a beat up Subaru!

Yes! Another stoplight. I like these the best.
I am gonna bark at that guy on his Harley in the black and orange biker vest!
I wonder where we are going? Anywhere is ok with me.
I just like to be King of the backseat and see what I can see!

I just love my owner. She treats me oh so well.

Brings me out to see new things and take in all the smells!

Something's up, moms upset. Looks like a wreck up ahead.

Looks like a Lexus got T- boned y an old Ford truck that's red.

Mom said it looks pretty bad. I will say a prayer that they are ok.

Then a thought came into mind in my mom's backseat that day.

We never know what's up ahead in this trip we have called life.

One minute things are going our way, and then there is trouble, heartache and strife.

Tell your loved ones you love them today, before the opportunity is past.

This ride called life is over really quick, only God knows which day is our last!

———————————

KING OF THE TRACK

I WENT WITH MY MOM TO THE PET STORE TODAY.
We needed dog food and new Frisbees for play.
When mom pulled into her parking place,
a man and woman were in each other's face.
Seems she had taken his parking spot.
These Christmas shoppers make a full parking lot.

Mom leashed me up and said, let's get in the store.
We headed in as she locked her doors.
On the way in I saw a strange sight,
six tall skinny dogs wearing harnesses so tight.
I heard a woman saying these dogs used to race.
This one right here was always in first place.

The woman explained they race on a track,
until they slow down, then they take them out back.
They're only needed when they're very fast.
As for these guys, their time has passed.
I looked in the eyes of the one called King.
Had that look like he'd lost everything.

I looked at mom like, "Can we help him out?"
She gave them a 20 and said, let's get in here and get out!

Once in the store, I heard a loud yell.
An argument over a collar with a bell.
Half priced collar causing a fight.
Grownups acting like kids, a terrible sight.

Mom found the Frisbees and dog food too.
A much larger bag than we usually do.
Got to the register, what a long line.
  Everyone complaining, we don't have much time.
Then a guy in the line made a fuss, threw a tantrum and started to cuss.
  Made the poor cashier lady cry, seems she had shorted him a dime!

I was tired of this and wanted to go home.
Into my own backyard, but I always roamed alone.
I had always wished for a special friend.
A lifelong buddy until the end.
Finally, we're about to get out of this place.
I hate going by the dogs with frowns on their face.

I'm going to trot by, not even stare.
"Mom! Why are you going over there?"
I heard her tell the lady, "People are selfish these days,"
Always about themselves and wanting their way."

These poor dogs have done nothing wrong.

Just slightly slower now, than when they once were strong.

I want that beauty that you call King.

We will spoil him rotten. Give him everything!

I looked at him. I swear I saw a smile that could light up a hillside for miles and miles.

Mom did the paperwork while he and I sniffed.

I call him, my Christmas gift.

Mom put us in the car. We sat in the back.

As she drove off, she tossed us a snack.

At the red light there was a homeless man.

Held a sign it said, help if you can.

Mom gave him money. We didn't get very far.

I saw him walk over and get in a brand-new car.

Then I began thinking of the bad things I saw,

the tears that were cried and the names that were called.

When I first saw King, my heart was sad,

but ONE act of kindness wiped out everything bad!

So, keep your light shining people. Be the one that does right.

It's good for your soul and helps you sleep at night!

Merry Christmas!

SCHOOL DAZE

IT'S THE STRANGEST MORNING EVER; not really sure what's up.
Trying to figure this whole thing out. I sure am one confused pup.
Everyone went to bed early last night; the kids were all in a bad mood.
Mom is up super early fixing everyone breakfast food.

Not really sure what is happening or what might even lay in store.
I am going to stay under the table and wait for bacon to hit the floor.
The kids are all wearing new clothes and brand named shoes on their feet.
Mom just tossed me some scrambled egg for an early morning treat!

The bookbags and backpacks are on the table.
The bathroom is busy as can be.
Grumpy kids in a really bad mood. What a sight to see!
No talk of riding bikes today or hanging out by the pool.
I think I finally figured it out! This must be the first day of school!

Mom is yelling hurry it up. She really is making a fuss.
What's that noisy thing coming down the hill?
Oh no, that's the kid's school bus!
Everyone's running out the door. Mom doesn't think it is funny.
Especially when she is running down the driveway yelling,
"Don't forget your lunch money!"

Finally, everyone is on the bus. The driver is shaking her head.
Probably wishing she was back at home relaxing in her bed!
Too quiet in this house today. Mom doesn't seem to mind at all.
I guess summer is almost over, giving way to the season called fall.

I hope the kids are doing ok at school.
Mom told them they would be fine.
What seems like hard times for them today are actually the best of times!!

REMINISCING

I REMEMBER THE DAY YOU BROUGHT ME HOME. What a lucky day for me.

I had no idea how special the rest of my life would be!

You are my best friend ever. We make a perfect fit.

You taught me all I needed to know like how to stay and sit.

You put up with a lot from me, back when I was a pup,

Like accidents on the carpet and those important papers I tore up.

Life is all about lessons, as I got older I learned;

you only corrected me because you loved me and used your voice that was firm.

For years you have spoiled me rotten. You put up with a lot from me.

Like the problem I have, I just can't resist, when you get up and I steal your seat!

I love you lying next to me, the feel of your gentle touch.

There is no way to thank you for your kindness, for me you have done way too much.

As I come to the end of my journey and my time is drawing near.

I want you to do one more thing for me, say goodbye with a smile and happy tears.

Remember our fun times together that we had right from the start.

You may not feel me lying beside you, but I will ALWAYS be alive in your heart!!

THE KITTY KLAUSE

Yes, I am a dog lover. I have two Border Collies and a German Shepherd. Before I owned any of them I had my cat. Some people love them, some don't, but my dogs wouldn't know what to do without mine! I hope this brings a smile. God bless you all! Thanks for reading this crazy stuff I write.

I HAVE THIS FRIEND. He's kinda strange you see.
He spends a lot of his time, up in the trees.
He doesn't make a barking sound. I guess it's more like a squeak.
One time he jumped on mom's waterbed and made it spring a leak.

This guy is always licking his self with his leg up in the air.
There is no way possible his tongue isn't full of hair.
He is a cross between a cactus and furry like a baby fox.
The weirdest thing about him is he poo poo's in a box!

The food they give him is delicious. It's better than mine any day.
Usually they feed him outside to keep me out of the way.
He has some really strange habits; there's one I don't understand the most.
He pulls out these ten little switchblade knives and sharpens them on a carpet covered post!

There's a sound he makes that drives me crazy; where it comes from really baffles me.
He sounds like my mom's car when she starts it, but I never have found his key.

Last night things got a bit crazy. My dad gave him something called nip.

He turned 14 cartwheels down the hallway and ended with a double back flip!!!

I just had to try some myself. It didn't do a thing for me!

But make my eyes red and watery and then I started to sneeze!

There's a secret I just have to tell you. While everyone's asleep, we cuddle at night.

I really shouldn't be telling you this, because dogs and cats are supposed to fight.

Mom said he is what's called a rescue. His family had to give him away.

Even though we don't always get along, I'm glad mom brought him home that day.

I wish everyone was like my mom. A huge heart of gold has she.

If we would ALL think of others instead of ourselves, what a wonderful world this would be!

ALL TIED UP

CAN SOMEONE COME AND PLAY WITH ME? I am really lots of fun.
I can fetch and catch a frisbee or go with you on your run.

I don't get much attention these days. A good grooming is something I
lack. I used to be the Apple of my owner's eye, now I am the dog tied up
out back.

I really don't know why things changed. We used to do so much
together. Now I am chained up to a tree, braving every type of weather.

My owner really is the best, only good words can I say.
He takes really good care of me, he feeds me *every* other day.

Maybe my barking got on his nerves. I guess that's one thing I could
change. My matted fur really itches me. They said I have something
called mange.

When my owner got this new girlfriend, changes began setting in.
He said she wasn't a dog person. I think I got under her skin.

I believe they broke up yesterday. I heard a really loud fight.
I was awake standing watch, guarding our house in the middle of the
night.

Look here comes my owner now, this is my happiest day yet.
He said he is taking me to the groomers, right after we go to the vet!

I am so glad to be with him. So tired of being alone.
Look what he tossed to me just now, a tasty beef marrow bone!

Human relationships falter no matter how much time you spend.
But a dog's love is unconditional, and we are faithful to the end!!!

HIS CHAIR

I DON'T KNOW WHERE MY OWNER WENT. Can you please help me find him sir?

He is kinda tall has real short hair and has camouflage colored fur.

I haven't seen him in three months or so. I remember him telling me bye.

He told me to take care of his family, and then he hugged me and said, "Love you big guy".

He told me to protect them with my life, that's why I am here with them at the park.

I stand watch and guard them daily from things that go bump in the dark.

Loyalty is my main attribute. I will be his dog until I die.

Bravery is my main characteristic. Please don't tell my family sometimes I cry.

My owner adopted me when he was fifteen years old. Nothing could keep us apart.

Then he started talking about something called the military, that thing called boot camp broke my heart.

He came home for just a visit, when his boot camp was done.

He spoiled me rotten for a couple weeks. Best time we ever had, man that was so much fun!

Next thing I knew he had to leave again. There went all of my joy.

But I must be strong I am here to protect his pretty wife and cute baby boy.

Don't try to come near either one of them. My jaws are real strong and I bite.

Don't think I don't love my owner's family, for them I would give up my life.

I guess that's what is ironic, to give your life for something you love.

That's what they say my owner is doing. Please watch over him, God above!

Everyone is acting strange today. Before we left his wife was decorating the house.

Friends and family had just come over; whispers were coming out of their mouth.

I even heard my owner's name, that kinda made me sad.

It made me think how much I love him and all the good times we had!

Well I really must be going. It was nice talking to you,

Back to the house where my family lives and a Persian cat named Ramsey too.

Almost to the driveway, this part hurts so much.

My owner would sit on the front porch with me. He always had the gentlest touch.

Sometimes I imagine I see him sitting on that top step.

I pray for him to come home soon, that would be the best prayer answered yet.

Strangely I smell his scent strongly today with all these people around.

I would know his smell anywhere; I must be part Bloodhound!

As I bust into the living room, someone is in his favorite chair.

Nobody sits in my owner's seat ever, I am gonna drag him out of there.

Good thing the back is towards the door. I can sneak up and make my attack.

Nobody sits in his chair; I will chew you up like a pupperoni doggie snack!

I turn the corner and slide on the rug. Look up and what do I see??

Oh my gosh, that's my owner, looking down at me!!!!

I jump up and straight into his arms with all four legs wrapped tight.

This is my owner I cry about in the middle of those long nights.

Thank you, God, for answering my prayers and keeping him safe from all harm.

Now that you are back here safe and sound, I am NEVER going to leave your strong arms!

TRIBUTE TO A WAR DOG

Dedicated to all military personnel past or present on two legs or four! Thank you for your service!

Chapter I

They took me from my Mom at eight weeks or so,
and brought me to this real secure place, but I really didn't want to go.
While other pups back home got to romp and play,
I was busy learning things like, Sit! Down! and Stay!

There was one guy they called my handler, I think his name is Mike.
He wore the same thing every day, on his arm was sewn five stripes.
He came and got me every morn before the sun was up.
Out of this place called the kennel, it was me and five other pups.

He would take me to do my business, then pat my head when I was through.
Sergeant Mike was a little strange; the other handlers were too.
Then my favorite time of day, when Mike would yell let's eat!
Me and the five other dogs, we were ready for our treat!

After all the food was gone, they would actually let us play,
Chasing ropes and balls and wrestling, what a way to start the day!
Then, it was time to get serious. We always knew it was time,
when they put a choke chain around our neck and made us stand in line.

They made us climb through tunnels and walk up wooden frames.

These army guys are kind of different, even more strange are their games!

After running this thing, they called the course, Mike would take me off with him,

To a metal building, marked explosives, it looked like an old gym.

They would hold this powder under my nose, then they would make me sit.

Then pat me on the head again, yelling "good boy, yes, that's it!"

I would do this every day, they said I was the best.

Then one day they took me out back, I wore a tan and brown camo vest.

As soon as I got back there, I started to smell that smell.

The scent that I was to sit down to, I knew it all too well.

Mike looked at me and said where is it boy? Go have a look around.

I found where the scent was really strong, they had it buried underground!

I sat down like they taught me to, to show Mike what I found.

Then I heard Mike scream out "yes!" He jumped three feet off the ground!

After three more months of this, I heard them say it's time.

They put me on a giant plane, me and this handler of mine.

The flight seemed like forever, I thought it would never end.

Then it was time to go to work, me and my handler friend.

This new place was dusty and everywhere was sand.

And everyone I was near had a rifle in their hand.

I heard them talking about me, said I was the best around.
Can someone point me to the water bowl in this sandy little town!
They didn't have a kennel there; Mike let me sleep at his feet.
Woke up before the sun came up, and he had me something to eat.

Then he said, "let's do this. We have a job to do,
We must clear IED alley, just me and you."
He took me to this dusty trail with piles of dirt everywhere.
He packed us a canteen of water, for he and I to share.
I smelled that smell that makes me sit. I knew it all too well.
Mike said, "find it for me, boy!" He was excited, I could tell!

I started on my journey, had my nose to the ground.
Barely had gone a half a mile and look at what I found.
There's that smell that makes me sit. It's what I am supposed to do.
Then Mike whispered stay right there, don't make another move.

Then at once a shot rang out, what was I to do?
Then it felt like my leg was on fire, Mike come and pull me through!
Mike grabbed me by my harness and held me to him tight.
He said, "bud you're going to make it, don't give up now, fight!"

He called someone on the radio, said, "we need help right away."
In flew a Blackhawk copter, he came to save the day!
First, he destroyed the snipers that put a bullet in me.
Then he hovered above us as a jeep came and helped us to flee.

I passed out from the blood loss, but then I finally came to.
Had no idea where I was, my leg I could barely move.

A guy they called the doctor said, you are lucky to still be here.
I just needed to know if Mike was ok, that was my biggest fear.

The doctor assured me he was ok, that wasn't enough for me.
Then I heard his voice, somebody open the door, I need to see!
There he was my very best friend. Then I tried to stand.
Then Mike tried to warn me, saying, "stay still if you can!"

The bone in my leg was shattered. It will never be the same.
They said something about a Purple Heart and a war dog hall of fame.
Yes, this shattered leg it bothers me, but compared to some this problem is small.
I was actually a lucky one because, many don't come back at all!

TRIBUTE TO A WAR DOG

Chapter II

Well, it's been 6 weeks now since I took one for the team.
That's what everyone is saying, I don't even know what that means.
All I know is I was doing my job, but I must have made someone mad.
Then that bullet went into my arm and made it hurt real bad.

I learned a lot about Mike that day. He was there shielding me,
from taking any more bullets, he is my handler you see.
After initial observations, the Doc said I'd never work again.
That made me so depressed, I need to protect my friend!

Then they called in a specialist, he said there might be hope.
Let him do my surgery, if he's the best, he gets my vote.
I heard them talking to Mike about what they needed to do.
Something about drilling and a metal plate and then a bunch of screws.

I thought they were building a dog house, or something off HGTV.
What I didn't realize is, those screws were going in me!
I didn't care; it was Mike's call. He always knows what's best.
As he huddled in a mini conference, with other men in tan and brown vests.

Next thing I knew a guy came in, a mask was on his face.

He lied and said this won't hurt a bit, they do that a lot in this place.

Then I got real sleepy, best sleep I ever had.

I had no idea what they were doing, when I woke up, it hurt really bad.

First thing I thought when I awoke was, I've got to try to find Mike.

I was worried about him. I had not seen him since last night.

Long story short, I got better. That doctor is the best.

They said I could go back to work, after something called therapy and rest.

After 4 weeks of rehab and learning that smell again.

I was ready for work. I needed to protect my friend.

Mike took me back out to the place with all the heat and sand.

Almost everyone there had a machine gun in their hand.

Then in the distance I heard that sound. The one that hurt me so bad.

Mike said, "it's okay boy". I trust him with all I have.

I overheard some talking. I think it was about me.

Something about being shell-shocked. I'll show them, just wait and see!

Mike took me out to the same place, where he had taken me before.

Then, I smelled that smell again. Time to make another score.

I located 13 IED'S that day. Mike was happy, I could tell.

Doesn't take much to make him happy. I just sit when I smell that smell.

Back at the camp, they were talking about a mission, to take place on the fourth of July.

Something about Taliban and Special Forces and getting Blackhawks ready to fly.

Mike told me I would be with him, when they go into battle that day.

Don't worry Mike, I'll protect you, and do anything you say.

Finally, the big day was here, and what a sight to see.

A long line of military vehicles and choppers to protect Mike and me.

They parked the convoy all in a row, on the side of the road.

Then they put me out front in what they call search mode.

I smelled that smell that makes me sit, but it wasn't underground.

It was coming from over that way with all those gunshot sounds.

Mike said hurry bud; we don't have much time.

We need to get behind that wall over there, then, we will all be fine.

I kept my nose down on that road, but didn't pick up a thing.

Finally, the smell got really strong, when I sat down Mike yelled "cha-ching!"

They moved everyone out of the way and brought in a special crew.

They were going to detonate it; they always knew what to do.

We stood back as we watched them, then, here came that sound.

Fireworks on the Fourth of July, the loudest ones around.

After the huge explosion, you just wouldn't believe,

hundreds of gunshots from over there, as far as the eye could see.

At once Mike started firing, there were bullets going every which way.

I just stayed as low as I could. Mike had told me to stay.

Then there was word that someone was shot. I knew that feeling too well.

Then that memory came back to me, that day was a living hell.

"We need to get him out of here," was what I heard Mike scream.
I guess there's another one, who took one for the team.
Then, there came a chopper. On its side was a red cross.
He came to pick up the guy that was hit and save a life from being lost.

Mike ran down to help him. He looked at me and told me to stay.
He told me to keep down low, out of the bullets' way.
Him and some guys grabbed a stretcher and strapped the guy on real tight.
And started carrying him towards the chopper, in the middle of this fight.

Then, I started thinking. I never got to sniff over there.
What if there's something in the ground that blows people in the air!
Mike and his crew made it; they got the poor guy in.
The chopper was up in the air, here comes Mike again.

I turned my head for a second to have a look around.
Then all of a sudden, I heard a terrible sound.
I took off running to where Mike was, even though he told me to stay.
Nothing else in the world mattered, except to see if he was okay.

I went where I last saw him, and I smelled him all around.
But, I couldn't find him anywhere, just his smell all over the ground.
Somebody help me find him! He has to be somewhere near.
Then a corporal picked me up with eyes full of tears.

Please don't take me with you, my best friend is out here lost.

I'm going to stay here and find him, no matter what the cost.

They put me in a chopper and took me back to base.

This must be where Mike is in that dusty dirty place.

They put me in my kennel and flew me way back home.

How is Mike going to get by, he never liked being alone?

Then, I overheard them talking. Someone named Mike had passed away.

Then I put it all together, and I fell on the ground that day.

Why didn't I protect him? He gave his all for me.

I should have been there with him and sniffed out that IED.

God, you don't know how I miss him, and all the time he spent with me.

But the one thing I learned from all of this, is the freedom we have in America is, anything but free!

TRIBUTE TO A WAR DOG

Chapter III

It's been over a month now, since I lost my very best friend.
The one I failed to protect up until the end.
I miss him so much it kills me. It really crushed my heart.
He was always beside me, right from the very start.

A lot of things have happened that I just don't understand.
I will try to explain it the best way that I can.
There was this box; in it was Mike's smell.
And a framed picture of him, that I knew all too well.

Draped over that box was an American flag.
And men in fancy suits, about Mike they would brag.
I heard a lot of whispers, as they walked by me.
Like that must have been his dog. Well that's pretty plain to see!

A lot of sad music was played on that day.
Then a man with lots of stripes had something to say.
On the front row was the family of Mike.
And one pretty lady, that he called his wife.

I met her one time. She came down to the base.
She looks different now with tears on her face.
There is something about her that looks a bit funny.
The first time I met her, there was no bump on her tummy.

I sat with the family, right by his wife,
as they all reminisced about Mike's life.
I felt Mike's presence around his wife that day.
Then we all bowed our heads and started to pray.

Then something happened that I don't understand.
Seven men appeared with guns in their hands.
Twenty-one shots went in the air that day.
It scared me so bad; I wanted to run away!

I guess that showed them. My war days were done.
Now I cringe every time I hear the sound of a gun.
I wonder what happens to me from here.
As we walked to the cars, I saw nothing but tears.

There goes Mike's wife. I hate to see her leave.
Beside her, I felt Mike's presence, inside of me.
Then you won't believe what happened that day.
How God intervened in a special way.

I heard his wife yell, "Can I please have the dog?"
A man in a suit said, "Let me check the laws."
While the man in the suit was on his cell phone,
out of her purse, his wife pulled a Milk Bone.

The man said there is a lot of red tape, but that she could take me on.
I can't believe this is happening, she is going to take me home!
The ride to her house was quiet. We had all been through so much.
She scratched me under my chin. I loved the feel of her touch.

Once we got home, she got out first. She said you wait right here.

She said something about another dog and a certain time of the year.

I didn't have a clue what she was talking about. I was just happy as could be.

To think I was with someone, who loved Mike as much as me!

Then I heard a dog barking. It was coming from behind a fence.

Then I caught this different smell; I haven't been the same since.

Then she yelled come on boy and put a leash on me.

Then the barking behind the fence got louder. I could hear it but couldn't see.

Then the gate was open, and what a big surprise.

A beautiful female just like me was right before my eyes!

I sniffed her through the kennel she was in, then she growled at me.

Mike's wife said, "don't pay any attention to her, she's in heat and this is day three."

Then she took me to my kennel it was really nice.

A house that looked like an igloo, but without all the ice.

"You two get acquainted", she said, while I get you something to eat."

Then she brought out two bowls of food, and marrow bones as treats.

As time went on, I adjusted. I really liked being in this place.

Each day Mike's wife's tummy got bigger, and there were less tears on her face.

I kept hearing talk about a baby, whenever her friends were around.

And lots of doctor visits, at an office that was downtown.

Then one night she came and got me and put me in her van.

She called me her personal bodyguard, don' t mess with her, I'll bite you if I can!

She said she had to run real quick to a place she called the mall.

I just liked being with her. I'm a guard dog and always on call!

When we got there, I didn't like it. She went in all alone.

Left me in the van with the motor running, windows cracked and with a Milk Bone.

She said she would just be a second. I had heard that before.

Women never take just a second in a mall full of stores!

I just sat there and watched for her and I saw her come out of the store.

Then I saw a large man approach her, as I tried to get out of the door.

Then, I couldn't believe it, that man had her around the neck.

My God, I need to get to her. It is my job to protect.

I tried to squeeze through the window, as I heard her scream my name.

I have got to get to her, or she will never be the same.

I slammed my head into the window, hoping it would break.

Now he had her by the hair. Now two lives are at stake.

I stood up on the armrest, and you won't believe what I found.

My back foot hit the button that brought the window down!

I flew out of that window and headed straight for him.

Remembering all Mike had taught me, those nights in that big gym.

I lunged with my jaws wide open and made a perfect strike.

He fell back, and I was on top of him, in that dark parking lot that night.

Mike's wife stood up as fast as she could and headed for the van.

Then she called 911, while I made minced meat of this man.

The police got there rather quickly, an ambulance came too.

They said she was lucky to have me. She could have been killed if I had not come through.

They took her to the doctor, and the baby was just fine.

He's just wanting out of there. By the size of her tummy, she doesn't have much time.

Then an awesome thing happened, in the hospital that night.

She went into labor and gave birth to little Mike!

I always felt bad about losing big Mike. I failed and didn't come through.

But now I get to make it up by protecting, his wife and Mike #2!

The bump on her belly has gone down now, since little Mike came into this world.

But now there's another bump on a pretty lady, the one in the backyard I call "My Girl".

Dedication

We come in every shape and size. All with one thing alike.
We love our furry four-legged friends, no matter what breed or type.

Hearts of gold are what we have for giving free homes to these pups.
While we take on more overtime, as the cost of feeding them goes up.

What is it that drives us to take them in, and let them rule our homes?
It must be those eyes, or the tilt of the head, while they feast on that new marrow bone.

They are great entertainment, I must admit, as I throw that ball again.
When he won't give it back, that kind of gets under my skin!

Then, there it is; he is in the stance. Yep he's making a poo.
As I walk around with bags on my hands, I do have better things to do.

Well his tummy must be empty now, I guess we better get something to eat.
Then maybe a bully stick, those are his favorite treat.

Maybe after that we can rest a while; all this work is wearing me out.
I'm tired from chasing you and cleaning up poop and throwing that ball around.

Gosh this dog is a lot of work; I don't know why we do it.
It's like he has a spell on me; there must be something to it.

Then one day I figured it out, exactly what it was.
That makes us sacrifice everything for these charming balls of fuzz.

I was feeling bad one day. I was dozing in my bed.
When I woke up, across my leg, I could feel a furry head.

He looked at me with those loving eyes, as I scratched him under his chin.
The love he showed me was magic! I was feeling better again.

This labor of love is hard sometimes, I know that this is true.
But if God ever allowed them to say three words, they would be I LOVE YOU!

Dedicated to all dog owners. Thank you for your labor of love!

ABOUT THE AUTHOR

Jerry Wayne Baldwin was born in Roanoke, Virginia and is the proud daddy of three sons and three dogs. Archibald Sky, (Archy) is a Black and White Border Collie that excels in agility and frisbee. Knuckles is a West German Working Stock German Shepherd and Kipper is a Red and White Border Collie who excels in waking the household up at 4 a.m. to herd imaginary sheep!

In addition to creating poems about our loveable furry friends that are enjoyed worldwide, Jerry also creates spirit filled devotional poems. Books with devotional poems are in the works. Follow Jerry at https://amazon.com/author/jerrywaynebaldwin to be notified when more poems are published.

Besides being a talented writer, Jerry plays guitar and accompanies his younger son, Zach who is very gifted in his own right on the piano. They provide music ministry at churches and events around Roanoke, VA in their Christian music group called Healing Reign.

ACKNOWLEDGMENTS

I would like to thank another dog lover, Shelley Atkinson. Without her, this book would not have been possible.

Shelley had read one of my poems on Facebook. She contacted me and told me the poem was so moving that I should write a book! I was a bit overwhelmed by the process and told her I would like to publish a book but needed some help. She kindly offered her assistance. She soon learned, as had I, that publishing a book isn't as easy as it sounds, but she stuck with it and here it is.

Shelley lives in south Alabama with her husband and assists her rescue dog, Trixie, with publishing Facebook, Twitter and website articles. Of course, Trixie doesn't type, so Shelley captures her thoughts for her. You can view her articles on health issues, product reviews and yummy recipes at https://TrixeTellsAll.com. Her Facebook and Instagram pages have the same title. Join her pack and you won't miss out on any information that will help you have a happy and healthy dog.

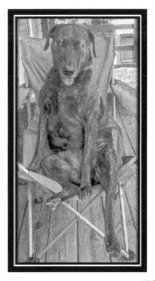

11136294R00049

Printed in Great Britain
by Amazon